short lean cuts
alex m. pruteanu

Copyright © 2011 by Alex M. Pruteanu

All rights reserved.
No part of this book may be reproduced or transmitted in any form or by any means, electronic or mechanical, including photocopy, recording, or any information storage and retrieval system, without permission in writing from the author.

ISBN-13: 978-1466244559
ISBN-10: 1466244550

Alex M. Pruteanu writes fiction at *Swine: ShortLeanCuts*
http://swine.wordpress.com

Book Design by Teresa Chapman

for you

instructions for reading short lean cuts

1. Pour a refreshingly-stiff libation of your choice; hilarity ensues within the next few minutes.

2. Please note the location of the exits on either side. If you are sitting in an emergency row you are required to prop open the door before you fling yourself first, down the inflatable inner tube slide thing. It's only fair to the trampling herd behind you.

3. Try to dedicate a chunk of time to read this book in one sitting. It is a very short book, but it flows better if ingested all at once. It shouldn't take you more than an hour and a half. Unless you're (Good) Will Hunting. In which case: how was it?

4. While in the ecstatic throes of the novella, don't, under any circumstances, answer the phone. It's that girl from The Ring with bad news for you.

5. Remember, this is *fiction*. It is made up. That's what writers do. Good fiction is truer than the truth. Ernest Hemingway once said something like that. But I have chosen to appropriate it because it sounds like something I would say, but couldn't come up with on my own. That's also what writers do: steal from everyone.

6. And finally: similarities to any characters in this book are purely coincidental…and quite unfortunate, really, for you.

(Grab here to begin fiction)

Contents

One	*(Quentin)*	1
Two	*(Cutter)*	4
Three	*(The Stink of the Business)*	7
Four	*(Distance)*	11
Five	*(Chinese Food Enlightenment)*	14
Six	*(Terminal Blocks)*	17
Seven	(Tramby Quirke)	19
Eight	*(Page 127)*	22
Nine	*(Sex Acts)*	24
Ten	*(Quick Dick)*	27
Eleven	*(Tramby Quirke Again Again)*	30
Twelve	*(Bestand)*	33
Thirteen	*(Cutting Weight)*	38
Fourteen	*(Proper Clipping)*	41
Fifteen	*(Good Therapy)*	45
Sixteen	*(Show Don't Tell)*	49
Seventeen	*(A Proposition)*	52
Eighteen	*(Trading Estate)*	54
Nineteen	*(My Caseworker)*	57
Twenty	*(My Caseworker's Notes)*	60
Twenty-One	*(I Don't Believe In You)*	63
Twenty-Two	*(Oui)*	65
Twenty-Three	*(Hospitals)*	67
Twenty-Four	*(Where the Story Ends)*	70

Interview with the Author   75

One
(Quentin)

The Ivory Tower manufactures different types of beasts. Usually these are physically benign but just as insufferable and effective as parasitic intestinal worms. What the usual gunsel wields to carve out your flesh, the Ivory Tower savage makes up for in the form of incessant circular chatter and philosophy.

Before I became the animal waste product that civilization shat out of its diseased, oozing asshole, I cut my gums for ten years in the Ivory Tower. Writing papers, I thought, was something I'd be good at.

Beware the bored academic with ambitions of prime time game show hosting.

Should I pick it up? I am looking at four hundred and sixty-eight pages filled with words typed in Times New Roman font. Size 10. Single-spaced. Two motherfucking spaces after the period. I am writing this with a red, hexagonal pencil courtesy of the

Office of Professional Development at Such and Such State University—the last thing I clipped before the Tower spat me out with a box of horseshit and trinkets in my arms. Should I pick it up? The manuscript needs a thorough autopsy. Attention. Kid gloves. I have consumed three-quarters of a gallon of Chianti table wine and it's seven in the morning on a cold Sunday in the South of something. Someone slipped a joint last night into the pocket of my bath robe. I roll it under my nose. It smells of prison and stale genitalia. Should I pick it up? The compressor has been laboring to kick on since 5:30. Sounds like a blue heron on its way through a manual grinder. Note: locate refrigerator warranty. Note: call for service between the hours of such and such. Central standard. Who the fuck telephones this early on a Sunday?

"Immiseration brings radicalization."

"What?"

"Remember the Deprivation Theory unit in Sociology 100?"

"I didn't teach Sosh."

"Well, listen. The Deprivation Theory speaks of inequality always begetting social upheaval, only somehow in this time we've all been pacified into some kind of reality-watching indolent monster who scratches his balls from time to time then feels good about causing a ruckus."

"Yeah?"

"We have been transformed into the greyhound chasing the electric rabbit and the faster we seem to run, the faster it gets away from us. We're walking blithely down the road to disaster. And yet the seismographs of public opinion show barely the faintest signs that we are preparing to redress what's been done to us. Are we not doomed?"

"I'm not interested in girl scout cookies."

"Are we not doomed?"

"Listen, can you fix a freezer compressor?"

"What kind?"

"Maytag."

"In 2005, Whirlpool bought Maytag and laid off 900 people, did you know that when you bought this defective piece of frozen shit?"

"Frozen no more."

"Semantics, you Philistine."

"Jesus, do you ever rest?"

"Let me ask you, when you are not in your apartment, does anyone have access to the food you eat?"

"What?"

"Polonium."

"What?"

"Fair warning, you snot-nosed hippie shit. Fair warning."

Then he hangs up.

Quentin.

He has tenure.

Two
(Cutter)

Things flow. We tap apps. Hit Save. The splicing is electronic. Shit happens somewhere in The Cloud. There's no chance anymore to guillotine the tip of your finger. Hit the bare bone. Expose it. When I was fifteen, I took a job as a movie projectionist at a chain of multiplexes. We sliced and spliced the emulsion, and held it together with clear tape. Careful not to mangle the soundtrack. 35 mm. Then 70. But the wide stuff came much later. At midnights on Fridays and Saturdays we ran skin flicks. Our most consistent clientele was a group of Chinese men who invariably travelled as a compact pack. They somehow moved seamlessly together, like protozoa using pseudopods. I fucked with them all the time. Instead of "Girls on Fire," I had our ushers lock the theatre doors, place cardboard into the small, slotted windows, and change the marquee above to "Grills on Fry." I watched the Chinese contingent sweat it out, moving from screen to screen, until one poor sap was forced to come up front and ask in which theatre the porno was slated to roll. If none had come forth, I'd have delayed the bastard. I made them ask. And got a kick out of the shame and humiliation they must've felt. Pulling on locked doors. Boners rising. Jesus, they're repressed in the Middle Kingdom. It's just porno, for Chrissake.

Sunday matinees were for kids. Cinderella. The Transformers. Lady and the Tramp. An American Tail. I fucked with them too. The parents. The grandparents. Children were collateral damage. I didn't care about children. I was fifteen. I'd splice a frame of porno into the middle of reel 2 of Ninja Turtles. Then watch it hit. One twenty-fourth of a second. "Ooo." I'd leave the soundtrack to the frame untouched. Or just lightly scratch it to garble it a bit. "Oghloo." Confuse the brain. One twenty-fourth of a second. Enough to register at the subconscious level. Shake up the crowd. The audio track ran alongside the emulsion in the form of a brown, thin bar. You could chip it with a sewing needle. A safety pin. Pocket knife. Leatherman.

Things have changed. We tap apps. Tap Save. It's called cutting; only it's not anything like that. It's just video games. Everything is video games. Lousy buttons and keys and wireless controls. Phone lines. Fiber. T1 lines. T3. OC3. OC12. 49. 192. Editing. ~~Strike that~~. (Which you can't. Not really.)

The other part is bad. The other kind of cutting. But I like it. I use razor wire or utility knives. Blades for shaving machines now come in neatly packaged triples or quints. The Gillette Mach 3. The Turbo. All fancy shit. None of it dangerous. None of it useful. I can't work with those. Just razor wire or utility knives. Broadhead blades. Hook blades. Pointed blades. Single-edged blades. Slitter blades. Slotted. Toothed. Even surgical blades. I shoplift them. They make blades out of tungsten carbide, stainless steel, carbon steel, titanium nitride, zirconia ceramic, ceramic coated. They're all good for carving through the thin layer of epidermis, into the flesh. The other kind of cutting. The self kind. The bad kind.

I'm no saint. I'm no sinner either. Just the worst possible human being you can imagine: I'm bored.

Three
(The Stink of the Business)

I'm cutting a filler piece called "Famous Flinches." It's meant to be a short, witty ha-ha for the 24:02 mark. It's a video omnibus of famous TV correspondents spasmodically ducking from incoming or outgoing artillery shells, mortars, collapsing light flags off camera pushed by hurricane-force winds, exploding or falling 1K Spots from studio grids, animals swiping violently at their mics, and a whole slew of other unimportant events which appeal to the segment producer in a perverse physical-comedy-meets-fear kind of way. Filler. It's all I do here. It's all everyone does anywhere. On the way to the toilet I am accosted by the insufferable, ironically-named Peter Joy. He's a freelance photographer with diminutive, soulless shark eyes, and a head twice as big as a bucket of horseshit.
"Where ya going? Got a minute?"
"No."

"Where ya going?"

"No."

"Listen, I got gold here," he says and pushes his Smart Device under my nose.

"No."

"I'm serious. Look."

He scrolls down through the menu on the little screen and double-taps an entry."

"No."

"Look. Look. I got Jim Vassar's home phone number."

"What?"

"Vassar's home phone. I got it. Right here."

He shows me a telephone number under an entry labeled: "Jim Vassar-Home."

"His home number. You believe it?"

"Joy, who cares?"

"Are you serious?"

"I need to piss."

"Are you some kind of moron? Jim Vassar's home. Home!"

"Fantastic, Joy. You can set up a date for the both of you to go have drinks and hash out his nightly news comment piece tonight. And maybe you can coax Ben Bradlee and Sally Fucking Quinn to join you. I also hear Woodward is available for a little romp in Georgetown. But later, after ten o'clock. He's busy, you know...writing books and talking to secret sources."

I leave him standing in the hallway with mouth open, incredulous at my indifference. Joy is a parasitic treadmill of a man. He's one of those cockroaches who roams the hallways, name-dropping and flashing the crooked, ignorant smile of a buffoon imbecile. What I really do best is remove stains from carpets.

Damp cloth. Always use a damp cloth.

Blot it. Don't rub the stain.

If you've ever cleaned a stain and had it reappear a day or two later, your carpet is suffering from wicking. This means the liquid has pooled at the bottom of the carpet. Even though you may have blotted up the initial stain, you only cleaned the surface. Eventually, the liquid works its way back up the fibers to the top of the carpet, causing it to look like the stain has reappeared. To prevent wicking, cover the area with a thick cloth and weigh down with books. Leave overnight and remove the stain by blotting.

Blot. Don't rub. Did you get that?

For stubborn protein-based stains, like semen, try rinsing with cold salt water first. Then go about tidying up the usual way. I know this from cleaning crime scenes after they'd been processed. It's what I really do best. The TV stuff is on the side. It's an offshoot of filmmaking. It's the compromise to my formal education.

Also this: bumblebees bite.

Only they cannot bite or gnaw through wood. Their jaws aren't strong enough. They cannot bite through skin, either. The thing about bumblebees is that they act as symbionts. They harbor parasites. They are also an excellent model system in which to study the evolutionary ecology of social insect-parasite interactions. Cuckoo bumblebee females, wax moths, trypanosomes, and Conopid flies all use the bumblebee in some way for laying eggs.

Parasites. Soulless.

Just like Joy.

It's all filler. All of it. Information, education, life.

We all are.

Four
(Distance)

Everything is laid out in the script. Down to the second. (commercial break: 2:02)

How I feel is, I'm a fresh aphthous ulcer being doused in pure lime juice.

How I feel is, I'm a paper cut drowned in salt water and Tabasco sauce.

There's a conversion engine which spews out surface distance based on coordinates you enter into its tiny Latitude and Longitude boxes. It also gives great circle distances between cities.

Here to Rabat: 4222.08 miles

Here to Damascus: 5656.73 miles

Here to Quito: 2323.03 miles

Here to Toronto: 798 miles

I enter Toronto again. Now it's 813. Strange. I've just gotten further by fifteen miles in three seconds. I open another tab in the browser. It takes me to AP. Reuters. Itar-Tass. AFP. FBIS. No, not FBIS. I once worked for that service. That's the CIA's "news and information branch." It doesn't exist. Which means I don't exist. So ~~strike it~~.

Mercopress. allAfrica. HR-Net. Then, finally CNN. They all run the same story.

"Smugglers Toss Hundreds of Refugees to Sharks"
Knife-wielding smugglers forced their passengers overboard off the coast of Yemen, so they could make a speedy departure after being spotted by Yemeni security forces. Four hundred and fifty people were dumped into the waters around the horn of Africa in the gulf of Aden. Twenty-nine people were confirmed dead—most eaten by sharks. Seventy-one are still missing.

Here to Mogadishu: 7619.68 miles

Here to Addis Ababa: 6954.96 miles

Here to here:

According to the engine, I am thirty-three miles away from where I'm dictating this. I enter the coordinates again. Thirty-three. This is the geographic version of Googling myself. "Hi, I'm Johan and I Google day and night."

I also enjoy domination, gag rubber balls, and tickling.

I'm very fond of women's feet.

Again. My own coordinates.

33.

Thirty-three.

Three-three, but now the number has a red asterisk in the form of a hyperlink. I click it. It's a Wikipedia entry for "Hades."

Also known as Pluto. The unseen one.

Here to Pluto: 2.7 billion miles. Roughly.

I try again.

Thirty-three miles away, only this time no asterisk. I'm always 33 miles away from where I am. North, south? Doesn't matter.

Someone ought to re-calibrate this engine.

(segment B, 4:05 followed by MOS {TRT: 1:19})

Five
(Chinese Food Enlightenment)

Right now what I crave is a menthol and a chemical peel. A tanning session. Electrolysis. Dermabrasion. My teeth capped. Liposuction. Calf implants. Botox. A pig's valve implanted in my heart. Angioplasty. I'm not self-centered. I just want to be sure that I'll be listened to and heard properly. Maybe even seen. Posthumous pictures. Those lovely little black and whites of happy families standing in front of the Grand Canyon. Mount Rushmore. Some ocean. An old-fashioned diner on Route 66. Maybe I'll be seen (the reason for the cravings). There's an odd chance. Right now my Television Q Score, if I were to be on television, is likely 0. I am ugly. I have dark circles under my eyes. The flesh on the face pulls down. I smoke. I cannot sleep. But I want to be changed. I'll have wanted to, anyway. I'll say I won't, but I'll want to, privately. It all counts toward something. It all counts toward the Q Score.

Adored.

A dord.

It has nothing to do with altruism, this record I'm leaving here. Nothing has anything to do with unselfish regard or devotion to others. The key to salvation is how much attention you get. You realize that there's no point in doing anything if no one is watching. You realize that if there'd been a low turnout at the crucifixion, they'd have rescheduled. You realize that if Jesus Christ had died in a hole, or some shit prison with no witnesses or no one there to mourn or torture Him, we wouldn't be saved.

I am as God created me. I am God's Son, complete and healed and whole, shining in the reflection of His Love. In me is His creation sanctified and guaranteed eternal life. In me is love perfected, fear impossible, and joy established without opposite. I am the holy home of God Himself. I am the Heaven where His Love resides. I am His holy Sinlessness Itself, for in my purity abides His own.

But throw these sentences at the mirror every day and see what happens. If you're not beamed out live over microwaves, it doesn't count. The glass shatters. Seven years of bad luck. Seven years of listening to yourself.

Or decades.

Whichever. No one listens. No one bows. No one hyperventilates at your words. No one is healed. It doesn't count. Sundays are for naught.

The mirror.

Reminds me of concave reminds me of converging reminds me of gorging.

Nobody wants to worship a fat messiah. Nobody wants to see an extra thirty pounds draped around your waist while you're preaching. Have you ever seen a fat Jesus?

How I feel on this machine, running endless miles and sweating off seven-hundred and fifty-three calories per hour, is like a ladder wrapped in nylon stockings under a giant heat lamp. Under duress, the revelations come at you from all directions. You're the tree falling in the forest and nobody gives a shit about it, because nobody sees it. You're the moon pie melting in the microwave oven. You're a nobody because nobody's watching you. These are the truths that swarm inside of you, running at nine miles per hour on a conveyer belt. And it's faux philosophy, Chinese food enlightenment, because you know that fifteen minutes after your head clears, you'll have forgotten it all. And crave it again.

Six
(Terminal Blocks)

Before I became this monster about to pull the plug on all that is inhuman and merciless, I worked at assembly lines in factories. Packing light fixtures into long, thin, cardboard boxes. Not unlike the job of a mortician. I volunteered at hospices and sat with dying men and women while they threw flattened ping-pong balls at empty walls and mistook me for their husband, son, father, uncle, cousin. I made up stories for them. I made up whatever they wanted to hear. Blue skies. Sparkling Ferris wheels. Nathan's hot dogs. Perfectly-weeded flower beds. Sucking toes. Suburban plots. I washed shit off old, naked, terminal men whose only mile-marker left in life was the next increment up in pain management. It never fails. We get there and turn to see who's come along, and no one's with us. It never fails. So I told stories for them. I don't want to connect anymore. Picking up phones at a sex-crisis hotline for two years

I heard various ways in which people tried to connect. There was a girl who called and said a policeman bullied her into having sex with him or he'd have charged her parents with abuse and neglect. He gave her gonorrhea. Her parents threw her out on the streets and she started living with male prostitutes in north Hollywood, picking up scraps from Musso and Franks' dumpster. At the end, she started crying into the receiver. I never knew if it was a true story. I said something something something. And it calmed her down.

I just don't want to connect anymore.

I drove you in disgrace from the mount of God, and I expelled you, O guardian cherub, from among the fiery stones. Your heart became proud on account of your beauty, and you corrupted your wisdom because of your splendor.

Seven
(Tramby Quirke)

I say, you've got to be kidding.

"Why?"

"Tramby Quirke?"

"Yes."

I tell her that sounds like a made-up name.

"They're all made up," she says. "Someone makes it up and gives it to you."

You know what I mean. It's straight out of Central Casting, I tell her.

"It is."

"I know it is." I tell her I once worked for Central Casting.

"As what?"

"Light tech and gaffer."

"How did you get your name?"

I say, when the doctor pulled me out with silver, cold forceps he

dropped cigarette ashes on my mother's thigh and changed her mind. The obstetrician decreed the birth a miracle. I was breech. I was inverted. He named me after a famous world conqueror. And a saint. That's the middle name.
Two saints really.
First and Middle.
She laughs.
"A conqueror and two saints. That's a mountain to live up to."
I tell her I'm apathetic. I tell her I don't believe in either. I tell her I don't just aim low. I don't aim at all. She says she knows. She jams the script against the stall wall and covers up the hole with Helvetica. Always Helvetica. Looks nicer.
"Remember?"
I say, I suppose we're in a relationship now. We should change venues. Meet up in other men's rooms. All over the city. I could bring flowers. Chocolates. Develop this further. I even ask for exclusivity.
"Exclusivity?" she says. "That's gallantly monogamous of you, Saint-Conqueror."
She snorts when she says that.
Tramby Quirke.
Quirky tramp.
And like that, she derails everything. Or delays it. She comes to me at the worst possible time. They all do.
She addicts me. I cannot let go of her.
How I feel is, I'm the female Red King crab caught up in a

gigantic pot full of males and they won't throw me back into the Barents Sea. They don't check for ovaries. They just leave me to suffocate. They leave me with dry gills. They rip out my articulating plates.

I'm the Opilio out of season.

"On page 127 we get married," she says. She moves the script around and I can see the scene. The dialogue. Fucking Helvetica. Always.

I say, what page are we on now?

"One twenty-seven."

Eight
(Page 127)

"Here," she says. "You can use this."

She rolls a plain, silver ring under the stall wall.

"Take it."

I do.

"Not yet," she says.

She hears what I think. I think. Or what I do.

And then she sticks her ring finger through the Glory Hole.

"Do you faithfully take me…"

I do.

"…Tramby Quirke…"

I do.

"…to have and to hold…"

I do.

"…in sickness and in health…"

I do.

And I do.

I slip the ring through the hole, onto her finger. I hear her tear off something. Then her toilet flushes.

I say, what was that.

"Page one-twenty-seven, is what that was."

I ask, where is that miracle she promised.

"I never promised it," she says. "I just said you needed one."

Fine. I need it then. Where is it? Tramby Quirke? Where is my miracle. But there's nothing anymore. She's gone. I look under the partition. No feet. No legs.

Tramby Quirke.

I walk out and take the elevator down nine floors. Ever notice how loud it is in an elevator? Beeps and clicks at each floor. Beeps when the doors open. Beeps when they close. Beeps when you push your number. Beeps when it beeps. Beeps when you beep. Beeps when you pick up the phone. Beeps when you stop. When you're stuck.

At the beep please leave your number.

I walk out through the lobby. Past the guard. The camera swings in a semi-circle and he watches on his black and white recessed screen. He buzzes me out.

Beep.

And I get my miracle.

Outside it's started to rain.

Nine
(Sex Acts)

On our seventh date, in the men's room of Nooshi on 19th and K-Street, Tramby Quirke shoots herself.
"It's not a date," she says from the stall adjacent to mine. "We're married."
I say I know. Page one twenty-seven. I say I remember, and turn the silver ring twice around the fourth finger on the left hand, in some sort of symbolic matrimonial allegiance to her. That's when she shoots herself.
"Oh you're so fucking dramatic."
She slides the Polaroid into my stall. It's a close-up of her pierced nipple. The jewelry gauge is thick and I ask her if it hurt when she got it perforated.
"It was a breeze," she says. "I was only going to get one done, but it was so easy and painless I got him to stab the other. My endorphins had run down, so the second was a bit more

painful."
She shoots again.
And says, "Did you know Egyptian Pharaoh Akhenaton, Roman Centurions, and some Victorian society women had pierced nipples?"
The flash cubes buzz for a second, then re-arm with an increasing high tone which bounces off the tiled floor then dissipates among the cavernous walls. I can smell the xenon gas. The picture appears under the partition. It's her fleshy tongue taking up the entire frame.
"Oh stop," she says, "if you could actually smell that, you'd be sniffing out E pills coming into Nogales for Godsakes."
I say I would never work for the government. She snorts. I smell the instant afterbirth of the Polaroid.
"Yea, instead you clean people's apartments."
I say I get paid under the table.
On the positive image of her tongue Tramby has scratched out "lick me" into the chemicals still developing layers of the film. The image is big enough for me to see the papillae—the small bumpy projections that hold the taste buds. They're white from dryness.
"What about my pussy?"
"No."
"Eyes?"
"No."
"Well. What do you want next?"

I say her feet.

Flash.

We're all miserable together.

"No," she says, "only you."

I ask her how she knows what I am thinking. She flips the pages of the script and hands me the Polaroid in between her painted toes. Then she asks if I want to be jerked off with her feet next time I'm cleaning a client's apartment.

Ezekiel, Chapter Nineteen, Verse Seven:

And he knew their desolate palaces...

Something something something. You can't keep the whole Bible floating in your head. You wouldn't have any room for girls like Tramby.

"Well, do you?"

I say yes.

Ten
(Quick Dick)

What shows up at the door is a flesh and blood incarnation of Alfred E. Newman. Only he's wearing tall, plumber's boots caked with dried excrement and mud, from having worked inside or around septic tanks. He comes in and bits of the dried shit fall off in the foyer.
"Yea, the filler float is done and you'll need a flush valve and a new handle…"
His language swirls around the bowl and I lose him. He's got his head in the toilet. He talks.
The bowl siphon.
The flush mechanism.
The refill mechanism.
Toilet function is based on gravity and siphoning. If you were to add water slowly to the toilet bowl, you would find that the bowl would fill to a certain level, and then stop; the balance of the

water you add, going down the drain. If you take a five-gallon bucket full of water and quickly pour it into the bowl, the suction of the water flowing out of the toilet siphons the water out of the bowl, leaving only a small amount of water behind. Many toilets are designed to have the water enter the toilet bowl through a series of small holes under the porcelain seat rim. These holes are angled slightly, causing the water in the bowl to swirl around. This swirling action, combined with the speed of the entering water, causes the contents of the bowl to quickly and thoroughly exit from the base of the bowl, into the waste pipes. Some modern toilets use variations on this theme, some attempting to accomplish the same task with less water. Some even use the pressure in your water line to accelerate the flushing action. I know this because I clean people's apartments as a side job. Scrubbing their toilets is part of the deal. It's in the daily planner they leave on their granite countertops in their kitchens.

14:45 hrs: clean master bathroom.

15:15 hrs: clean guest room.

I make a joke about his name.

With a straight face he says Quick Dick is the company's name.

That's not a name tag. It's the logo.

Then I tell him about Tricky Dick Nixon.

Haldeman.

Ehrlichman.

Frank Sturgis?

John Mitchell?

He chews gum and sucks on his teeth.

He tells me the story of a client who was deathly afraid of flushing toilets, so the guy pissed into large, plastic jugs which he would empty at night into the sewer across the street. I say, what about his fecal matter.

"His what?"

I say, his shit.

"That's the thang," Alfred E. Newman says and sucks on his front teeth. "His commodes done got clogged with all of it he wouldna flushed. That's where I come in." He slaps his thigh and explodes into laughter. The slapping shakes loose another piece of dried muck from his boots.

I say, I can't imagine the mess.

"Pfft, at's nuttin'. Once this man called up from…"

How the story goes is, another client's septic tank hadn't been maintained for years and the broken down components of wastewater came back up the toilet while the man sat comfortably and read the results of the previous day's ballgames.

How I feel listening to Alfred E. Newman spew his excrement about his trade is, I'm the anaerobic bacteria which he's now describing: I'm breaking down.

Eleven
(Tramby Quirke Again Again)

She says, "Shhhh....it's sleepy time."

"What?"

"Sleepy time."

"What's sleepy time?"

She says, "Quit the gear."

I say, I can't. I'm part of the Cult of Agriculture Fertilizer.

She snorts: "And I drink the Kool-Aid. Please. Just quit the gear."

"I can't. I'm addicted."

"Shhhh…it's sleepy time."

"It's absurd."

She says, what.

"All of this."

"I'm going out to get something to eat. I'm low on sunflower seeds. Need anything?"

I ask her to pick up some cleaning products. I've got a gig in Watts day after tomorrow.

"You really ought to think about quitting this," she says.

I say, I can't. I'm addicted. I'm addicted to her.

Only I don't say that part. The last part.

"No, not that. This."

She makes a scrubbing motion in the air.

I say, fuck.

"What?"

I cut my scalp.

"Silly. It says on the box: DO NOT USE WITH A RAZOR."

"So what now?"

"I'm going out."

"Pick me up…"

She says, cleaning products. "I got it."

"No."

"What?"

"Band-aids."

"The wide kind?"

I say, yes.

She grabs the box of depilatory cream.

She says, "Jesus. This is for black men. To shave their faces with."

I say, is it.

"DO NOT USE WITH A RAZOR."

I say, story of my life.

"You have no life."

"I have a fetish."

"I know. The feet…"

"No. My filing system."

"You have a system for filing your nails?"

I say, no. Just papers and receipts.

"From whom?"

"Employers. W-2s. Baggage like that."

"I thought they paid you under the table."

I say, they do lots of things to me under the table.

She snorts.

On her way out she tosses back: "You should really try to sleep."

I tell her I don't sleep.

"Don't take the 405 if you leave. Some Goth kid jumped off the overpass into traffic."

"How do you know?"

She rolls her eyes. And then she's gone.

Twelve
(Bestand)

I stole this word. It's not mine and it never would have been had Martin Heidegger not banged out his ideas on some musty Underwood in a comfy study of a spacious enclave in Freiburg. All right, I made that up.
The Freiburg part.
Heidegger pointed out how human beings tend to look at the world as a standing, giant warehouse stocked with material ready for them to use; simple inventory available to be processed into something more valuable.
Bestand.
Beans ground down into a fine-powdered espresso blend.
Trees into paper.
Animals into food.
Products processed from natural resources.
Temperature bottled into giant cans and sold at exorbitant retail

prices.

For those of us without access to the heavy-duty inventory like oil wells, diamond mines, natural gas pockets eight miles below the Gulf of Mexico, it seems evolutionary to utilize the only thing we can tap.

Our lives.

Our own intellectual property.

Our experiences as product.

What Heidegger points out is the tendency to translate Bestand into exploitation and enslavement for our own benefit.

And so this is what this is. This story. It's a shameless exploitation of my life; where everything becomes manufactured with a purpose: sell it to you.

Make money.

That's what my agent wants.

Careful now.

If a tree falls in a forest…

The problem with this is that we shape events by just being there. Observing.

If a tree falls in a forest…

We note it all down and tweak the tale for dramatic tension. Exaggerate and change around the past until the real line of events disappears. History becomes inaccurate and we forget who we are. All we hope is that this becomes the next great vehicle for Miss Twenty Million Dollar a Picture Movie Star. Experiences manufactured and lived for the sake of a marketable story. It is possible to exploit yourself for that. It is possible to enslave yourself for it. It's certainly sensible to enslave others for it.

Acceptable, even.

This is what this is. This story. My story. There are a million of them out there. Much more dramatic than this. They're all skillfully disguised as therapy.

Just like this one is.

Tweaking and editing for the sake of a Hollywood screenplay, all the while trumpeting the cathartic powers of the confessional. How I feel is, I'm the sucker who just shelled out fifty bucks for a seven-minute session in a miniscule booth in some lobby of a second-rate hotel in Des Moines with an assistant of an assistant to an editor at Talk Miramax, willing to listen to my processed life story.

Deli meat.

Head cheese.

You've got seven minutes to exploit yourself before the line moves up one person. And another. And another.

Go.

It's a bit like soliciting a prostitute. Your girl is giving you seven minutes to come.

Go.

It's a bit like weekly confession. Your priest is giving you seven minutes to spew and atone.

Go.

And right smack in the middle of your third act in which you triumphantly and ceremoniously traverse drug addiction, divorce, depression, pregnancy by rape, incest, terminal illness…right before the big bang…

Your seven minutes are up.

Next in line is another copy of you clutching the fifth and final draft of his polished screenplay. Fifty dollars to pitch your life to a bored publishing functionary who will collect his fee and get comp-ed for that basket of fruit and wine in the Executive Suite of the HoJo in Lind, Washington.

The story no longer follows the experiences. All events happen in order to generate the story.

And always the next guy will upstage you.

One-up you with his Sunshine and Singing Birds and My Dad Is on Top of Me screenplay.

Careful now.

The line has morphed into research. Experiences as research. Hitting kiddie-porn sites in order to do research for a sexually abusive autobiography.

Shoplifting at a high-end store in Beverly Hills to prepare for an upcoming role in somebody else's therapeutic narrative of triumph over kleptomania.

This is what this is. A record of the ills of Bestand. It is the only fingerprint of an insignificant life spent chasing cars and sniffing their exhaust. Seeking notoriety and acceptance into society by metaphor and hyperbole and redemptive self-flagellation. In act three, I fall in love with a girl with blue eyes. Tramby Quirke is flushed down into the pipes underneath the city and just then… Your seven minutes are up.

Sorry, but.

Thirteen
(Cutting Weight)

As in wrestling. Not that kind—the entertaining kind. Not that one. Inflated pecs and overblown calves. Bleached blondes. Mullets. Shaved heads. Silicone tits. Accusations and inflammatory rhetoric in giant arenas. Not that one. Greco-Roman. Freestyle. 54 kilograms. 120 Ks. That kind. It's the most excruciating sport. The oldest. Grueling training sessions punctuated always by demonic and frantic methods of losing weight. Making the right weight. I once had a job supervising an indoor, air-conditioned track in Skokie, Illinois. Mostly, it was used by geriatric patients trying to extend their lives a bit, walking around and around in an attempt at a healthier end. But peppered among the quickly dying were wrestlers running in tight, silver body suits, spitting into cups every lap, trying to drop those last 5 pounds before weigh-in. Cauliflower ear. To most amateur wrestlers, it's like a tattoo. A rite of passage. An entrance into the club. Fight Club. The first rule of Fight Club is. You get cauliflower ear from constant rubbing. The cartilage separates from the skin and blood and fluid builds up. After a while it drains out, but the calcium will solidify on the cartilage. You have to drain it. Most guys use their own needles. The ear fills up with blood and you have to drain it before the blood hardens. A doctor can do it, but you have to go in there all the time, so guys just purchase their own needles and puncture themselves. I used to know a boy who would punch himself ten times just before bed, to get cauliflower ear. One of the guys sweating it out at the track had a massive injury from wrestling which required a re-built human valve for his heart. He decided against the pig valve, the better choice, because a re-built membrane allowed him to wrestle again. It's membership into an exclusive club. No one comes to see wrestling. Guys do it for the high. It's an addiction. Everything we do is an addiction. Living is an addiction. Dying is. Amateur wrestling is the ultimate analogy for the former. It's a cult. A fraternity. Family. Wrestling is life. There are a million decisions to be made in seventeen minutes. Seventeen. 17. Do you hear that number? The mat is your life. I hate internal blood. ~~Strike that~~. Blood from failure of internal organs. I can't explain this. All blood is internal. All blood is equal. But some blood is more equal than other. I used to run. Once I ran eight miles per day for sixty-eight consecutive days. At the end, when I came inside to piss, blood came out instead of urine. Then it would coagulate and a little later I'd go to piss again, and a tiny sliver of red scab would come out of my urethra before the blood flowed again. Crimson. Beautiful life. The doctor couldn't figure out anything. He gave me an antibiotic and I was off. But I knew what had happened. I had jarred loose the prostate from running. I never had the body for running. Internal organ blood. It's different than cutting yourself with a blade. Some blood is more equal than other. Blood as product. Blood as cleanser of human waste. An old wrestling ritual to mark the last match of one's career goes like this: you leave your shoes in the center of the mat and cover them up with a handkerchief. Then you kiss the mat and leave the shoes behind. The wrestler with the re-built valve, jogging around the indoor track, dated Walter Mondale's daughter in Ceylon, Minnesota. She left him when he broke his sternum. When he herniated his disk between C5 and C6 of his spine. Hyperextended knee. Hyperextended elbow. Broken hand. Broken finger. Broken clavicle. Dislocated shoulder. Severe tear in the back muscle. She left him. He never left wrestling. It's a fraternity of broken men. It's Fight Club. The pain is what keeps the fans away from the stands. No one comes. Just family. Wives. Brothers. No one comes to see wrestling. No one wants to see life played out on a mat. No one.

Fourteen
(Proper Clipping)

To shoplift a small, 6-pound can of freon, you wear a ten-gallon cowboy hat on Halloween into the store and deftly deposit your "miracle compound of CFCs" (to be inhaled only) on top of your head. Everything nice and neatly obscured by your costume. Walk out.
Rinse and repeat and repeat.
To shoplift anything, take off the tag and run it to the Lost and Found. Then come back a few days later and claim it. It'll still be there.
I once shanked a rare coin collection from a friend, pawned it, then booked to Shakey's and hit the all you can eat pizza buffet. Morals are my weak spot now. It used to be bad taste.
Happy Cruelty Day, you.
The best remedy for being blocked is counting calories.
In my feeble attempt to leave behind The Story for The Agent for

The Star for The Oscar for the TV Ratings for the Advertising Revenue for the Network Profits, what I've managed to do is deconstruct everything to its nutrinos.

Weak force.

Gravitation.

Electrically neutral lepton.

When you strip something down to this elemental level, you can no longer see the big picture. Whatever that may be. That's for my caseworker to decipher. She's writing all this down, as I'm dictating it into the Grunding reel-to-reel. (She writes: Luddite) She says, Jesus they make little pocket sized tape recorders nowadays.

I tell her to piss off and start shaking. Part of her job as my caseworker is to mix me a gin martini. She and I have become good friends.

But I promised you advice for elementary clipping.

Here we go.

Wear baggy clothing. Much easier in cooler climates. Make sure to choose a coat with inside pockets.

Pick the right store/merchandise. Hit the large chains. Mom-and-Pops defend their territory with a vengeance. Go small on the merchandise, but valuable. No one's going to be impressed if you lift a head of garlic. Hit CD ROMs, cell phones, digi-cams, iPods, memory chips.

Misdirect.

This is a magician's skill that comes in handy when shoplifting.

(Most professional magicians don't pay for anything. The rest, are just plain bad. You can see the fishing wire in the lights.) What you want is to select the item you wish to take with you from the store. Position yourself near it, and then pick up a different item. Hold this second item up, look at it in the light, lick it if you want to, just so long as anybody watching you do this is observing your actions with this particular item. Meanwhile, your other hand is grabbing the object you actually want and slipping it into your coat pocket.

Fooling the sensors.

There are a great number of ways to get past the door sensors. Understand first that what the sensors are looking for are electronic tags on the merchandise. The first thing you should do before slipping your prize into your pocket is identify the security tag. Pulling it back out of your pocket to check is not recommended.

Subheadings:

The courtesy sensor.

This is when the sensor is not directly in front of the door, and customers are just expected to know to walk through it. Just don't walk through it. Or, if you are under surveillance, start to walk through it, and then drop your keys on the outside of the sensor. Lean over to pick them up and then walk around.

The friendly counter-person.

Often, there is a pad near the register that deactivates security tags. Find a friendly counter-person, start up a conversation, and

ask to see something behind him. Lean over to point at what you're interested. When his back is turned, rub your pocket against the deactivation pad.
Security.
Things to know.
Shoplifting is against the law.
You'll probably get zapped by six different cameras doing the above. The trick is figuring out which ones are real or fake. Most of those hideous-looking black orbs hanging from the ceiling are fake. Most stores have them. They're props. Most working cameras are watching middle management making deposits in the office. Watching the safe. The watchers watching the watchers watching the watchers watching us. And think this. Cameras cannot catch you. Employees will. Tape is only used for proof.
You'll probably be prosecuted if you're clipping anything over two hundred. You'll probably get sixty-five to one hundred hours of community service, but incur about two grand in lawyers' fees and court expenses. You'll probably need a third job to pay off all of those. Which doesn't leave anything for anything. Not even enough bile. Which brings you back to clipping things.
How you feel is, squeezed to a fine powder in a giant vise.
EXODUS 20:15: *Thou shall not steal*.
I'm tired of the Bible.

Fifteen
(Good Therapy)

After all this, you won't catch me around. Bit up. Bit up. Chin up. I will be a case number in someone's folder. Letters on a headstone or ash in a tube. You won't care a bit. There will be a spike in ratings. There will be three days of filler on the cable news networks. They will squeeze the blood out of the fact that one of theirs has done what he has done. On television. And highly unlikely, but possible, there will be a reality show made of it. Someone will produce. Some other one will judge. They're all ants. They love the grease AND the molasses. And nothing will go down into immortality. Movers will come and haul away the trains and sewing machines and in their place they'll leave oil-stained floors and open-ended wave guides excited by electric currents.

All that matters is Nielsen ratings.

Product placement.

Advertisements.

My caseworker is a young woman. About twenty-something. Straight out of University. She smokes my menthols. She kills my Scotch. Part of her job is to mix me a gin martini when she comes by with her notebooks and tape recorder and weekly planner.

And.

The DSM.

Diagnostic and Statistical Manual of Mental Disorders.

The DSM has gone through five revisions since it was first published in 1952. The last major revision was the DSM-IV published in 1994, although a "text revision" was produced in 2000. The DSM-V is currently in consultation, planning and preparation, due for publication in approximately 2012. Mental health professionals swear by the DSM. They swear by the APA. What most people don't know is who else uses the DSM.

Insurance companies.

Exploiters of usury.

Part of her job as my caseworker is to dirty up the concoction with olive juice.

Part of her job as my caseworker is to note progress.

I humour her. We go through like this together and I miraculously find my cathartic vehicle, and every session I open up nonexistent emotional inner vaults housing the psychiatric version of contraband and illegal product made in China. Twenty-first century tweaking with pills and hypnosis and therapeutic boo-hoo-hoo.

Need a tissue?

Part of her job as my caseworker is to light my cigarettes.

Part of her job as my caseworker is to diagnose me with a new disorder or phobia every week and document it thoroughly in her paperwork. Her folders.

Part of my job as her case number is to entertain her useless degree.

In one month I've switched from bi-polar to manic-depressive to agoraphobic. Over the past hundred and sixty days she's filled her notebook pages with:

Ablutophobia—fear of washing or bathing.

Acousticophobia—fear of noise.

Cacophobia—ugliness.

Nebulaphobia—fear of fog.

Proctophobia—fear of the rectum.

"Are you homophobic?"

I say, no.

She scribbles words into her printed form.

"Are you sure?"

I say, yes.

And we're on to the next batch.

Melanophobia—fear of birds.

Bromhidrosiphobia—fear of body odor.

Bogyphobia—fear of the Bogey Man.

I like that one. She says, "Don't give me that smile."

Merinthophobia—fear of being tied up.

She raises her eyebrows at that one.

And we go like that until when?

Until what happens?

Bolshephobia—fear of Bolsheviks.

Taurophobia—fear of bulls.

Coimetrophobia—fear of cemeteries.

Wrong. I've always loved them. I once read a book over satellite phone to a girl with blue eyes, in a cemetery. In another country. But I've locked that. That one is for me. I won't tell you about it.

Coitophobia—fear of coitus.

Agiophobia—fear of crossing streets.

And so we go until…

Sixteen
(Show Don't Tell)

…so now I show up to work with a bucket of chemistry, medicated. If I come to work at all.

"Didja sleep?"

I have my days to burn through.

"How long?"

…so now I have to combine Eszopiclone and Triazolam to log in at least three or four hours of scrubbing. Only both of these are un-safe: Have you a history of alcohol or drug abuse? Depression? Lung disease? A condition that affects metabolism? Pregnant? Have you a history of kidney or respiratory problems? Sleep apnea? Are you breastfeeding? Suicidal?

Yes.

Then what I need is Estazolam–a benzodiazepine derivative. Un-safe for older adults. May interact with other medications. My caseworker says it will help me stay asleep. Only I take it with Amitriptyline.

"You using any MAOIs?"

I tell her I've been recovering from a heart attack.

She writes in black ink on pre-lined forms.

Trazodone. But it interacts with Warfarin and other herbal supplements.

She says. Are you taking any herbal supplements?

Saw Palmetto.

For?

Prostate issues.

My caseworker as a nosy, snooping around private dick.

"You die because you sin."

What?

My caseworker. She's a Christian. "What else?"

"What else what?"

"I need something for blurred vision, constipation, dizziness, prolonged drowsiness, weight loss. No. Weight gain."

"Those are all side effects."

"I have them."

My caseworker. She writes with impunity, pushing down hard on the forms.

"I can't prescribe anything out of the DSM," she says.

Jesus. I scratch behind the ear.

Jesus.

"What?"

"Nothing."

"No, what?"

Jesus.

"What? What is it?"

I realize.

I'm too fat for this kind of Jihad.

Seventeen
(A Proposition)

Tramby Quirke says, "If you could have her back for ten minutes, which ten would you choose?"
She offers this carrot in the washroom of Amedeo's after the head waiter walks out without cleaning his hands with soap.
What he is to us, is a pair of black trousers from the knees down, whistling and pulling open the door with a whoosh.
Like the suction in hotel rooms when you walk out into the hallway.
What you don't know is that I had a child who perished at the hands of a man behind the wheel, looking down at a set of directions written on paper on the passenger seat next to him. He swerved. And didn't adjust. What he left for me was a reflection of a girl in a car window, which always moves right to left when I pass. Sometimes we cross. But never do we walk together. Not even briefly.

"Which ten minutes would you choose?"

What.

"Would you have her back as a little baby, a dirty-faced toddler, a schoolgirl, a student just completing her baccalaureate, or a young woman going off to live?"

Tramby is ruthless. I tell her that. She asks me again.

I say, let me have her when she was six and in a moment of anger she doubled up her fists and shook them at me and banged them on my chest and said I hate you, I hate you, I hate you and in a little while her anger subsided and she collapsed on the floor and cried and said I'm sorry Dad I didn't mean it. I didn't mean to say I hate you. And she sobbed because she felt guilty for saying that. And I felt guilty for letting her feel guilty.

Let me have her back for those ten minutes, I tell Tramby. There is something I need to do. Something I can do.

Will you let me have her?

But she's gone. She's always gone.

Ruthless.

Eighteen
(Trading Estate)

Odd faces are buried in horizontal walls. Schopenhauer leans in, blows a contemptuous kiss, and smooths over his mutton chops. He says, I told you so. Dali twists on the left side of his moustache and does a killer El Greco. Einstein floats in zero G. As Gandhi steps aboard a train one day, one of his shoes slips off and lands on the track. He is unable to retrieve it as the train starts moving. To the amazement of his companions, Gandhi calmly takes off his other shoe and throws it back along the track to land close to the first. Asked by a fellow passenger why he did so, Gandhi smiles. "The poor man who finds the shoes lying on the track," he replies, "will now have a pair he can use." How I feel is, I'm the little kid in that movie who sees dead people.
"Where did you go?"
"I left you because you were getting soft."

"That's quite a radical version of letting me cry it out."

"That's melancholy for you."

"You dangled a carrot."

"I asked a hypothetical question. You cannot separate that?"

You started it.

And you finished it when you should've gone on.

And we're in fourth grade on the playground shoveling sand into one another's eyes.

Tit for tat with Tramby. In exchange for three hounds and a handful of sea salt thrown over the left shoulder, Tramby lets me help her dissect cadavers and prepare them for medical students to dismember in the morning. She opens up the chest of a sixty-two-year-old doctor whose muscle mass is that of a man in his twenties.

She says, hold here. I keep lateral pressure on both sides of the breast plate, pulled apart, while she digs her hands into the man. She says, "I need to pour in Formalin. To make his lungs float." And she does.

Coils and wires appear from within. His pacemaker. His heart is the size of his head, almost.

Anadrol.

Anabolic steroids.

She says, no. Dianabol.

She says, "This guy must've downed ten pounds of egg albumen every day of his miserable life. God, look at the size of his nuts."

They're marbles.

I know Tramby from Polaroids. This is me angry. This is me troubled. This is me happy. This is me sleeping. This is me low. High. In between. I have a book full of Tramby's emotions shot on self-processing emulsion. It's the only way I've gotten to know her. Before, I'd be astonished at how different she'd look in every photo. And then I realized that I'd never seen her in the flesh. I'd never seen her react. So I made her shoot herself at different emotional stages. I made her shoot herself.

With Polaroids.

But you knew that from before. I'm starting to repeat myself.

Early stage of senility.

What this is, is a pond. It doesn't go anywhere. It stagnates and eventually evaporates.

We trade estate for a bowl of lentil soup.

She and I.

Nineteen
(My Caseworker)

I say, "Suicidal? Let's not jump to anything here."
She scribbles in black ink on pre-printed forms.
"So…then you have some kind of timeframe in mind?"
Instead of answering, I guide her down a tangent about removing household mold stains. She loves perceived challenges like that. She's trained to read between the lines, only between my lines there's nothing. There's just white space. White noise. Bleached paper.
"Cosmic radiation," says Tramby Quirke. "Part of TV snow is cosmic radiation."
She's sneaking into my conversations now like Ben from Death of a Salesman.
"Ben?"
I say, yes Ben.
"Ben?" says the caseworker. "Who's Ben?"

"Who's Ben," says Tramby.

What?

"Who's Ben," says my caseworker.

"Yea, who's Ben?"

I say, Tramby?

"Who's Tramby?" says my caseworker.

I say, Ben. From Death of a Salesman. Willy's brother.

"Tramby's Ben?"

I say, no. No. Ben is Ben. Tramby is…

The caseworker scribbles into her forms.

I say, Tramby?

"Who in hell is Tramby?"

"Yes, who in hell is Tramby," Tramby laughs.

"Are you all right?"

What.

The caseworker. Right.

Cleaning grout in between ceramic tiles.

What people don't know is that rubbing alcohol does the same job on mildew as the expensive products. Mildew requires two things to survive. Moisture and lack of air.

My caseworker scribbles down notes.

Mildew as a metaphor for disintegration of the human psyche.

Mildew as a metaphor for rotting on the surface and below.

Lack of air. Asphyxiation. Suicidal tendencies.

I say, electric elbow grease. There's a tool with a triangle-shaped head that you can run for a few minutes on the grout. It vibrates off the fungus without the use of product. No need for proper ventilation.

"And anyway, you're running low on gin," she says.

I say, Tramby?

"Who in hell is this Tramby?"

"Nothing. She's no one. I don't know though."

She writes furiously into her notebook. Then opens up the DSM. This week: prepsychotic phases of social and academic/occupational impairment.

The beginnings of Schizophrenia.

If untreated, fifteen percent of individuals with Schizophrenia commit suicide. However, antipsychotic medication usually prevents suicide, minimizes rehospitalization, and dramatically improves social functioning. Unfortunately, even on antipsychotic medication, most individuals with Schizophrenia can't return to gainful employment due to the intellectual impairments caused by this illness.

This is why I clean people's apartments.

Twenty
(My Caseworker's Notes or Writing Through Lists)

You can smell it. The difference between TNT and the plastic: RDX, Semtex, C3, C4.

C4 is what they used to blow a hole into the Arvada nine years ago. You can smell the difference. You can feel the difference in rehearsals. The vibrations within your bones are indescribable. They make you touch them.

Electronics.

Sniper.

Testing for batteries.

Fuse construction.

Boom-boom vests.

You poison dogs and you watch them die. You hit them with nerve agents and watch them struggle in their cages.

Sarin.

Phenothiazines

Organophosphates.

They gas you as well, and then you take Atropine and anticholinergic drugs because they block acetylcholine receptors, but they are poisonous in their own right.

2-PAM chloride is the best antidote. It reactivates the poisoned enzyme acetylcholinesterase by scavenging the phosphoryl rest attached on the functional hydroxyl group of the enzyme. It's safer to use, but takes the longest to act.

Choose your poison.

(Hey, choose your poison! Remember next time you hear that, make the right decision.)

Novichock Agents. "Newcomer" in Russian. A series of organophosphate compounds that were developed in the Soviet Union from the 1970s to the 1990s.

Designed to be undetectable by standard NATO chemical detection equipment and to defeat chemical protective gear.

There are forms to sign. There are always forms to sign. No matter where you go. Pre-printed rectangular boxes. Blank lines. Bureaucracy seeps into everything you do. Including the lucrative business of dying.

More courses: propelled weaponry, military-grade sophisticated equipment, international operations, mass transport, defense against enemy drones.

But there is accounting: incurred costs.

Accelerated depreciation.

Misstatements.

Patronage dividends.

Phantom Income.

The decentralization of all structures has created costs passed down to all the hapless cogs.

My caseworker is one of those glass half full types.

She believes in cognitive behavioral therapy.

Interpersonal therapy.

Psychodynamic therapy.

Group.

Electroconvulsive.

My caseworker is a Creationist. She believes the earth is five thousand years old. She believes in lists and cross-referencing and diagnosing from the DSM. You cannot argue with people like that. You can only set yourself off among them. The end of something is always the beginning of something else. I know. Not exactly Kierkegaard.

Twenty-One
(I Don't Believe In You)

And all I'm left with is the taste of foreign spit and blood.
I tell her, when the punches came, it wasn't unlike my father's belt crashing down on flesh, splitting the skin like blade on silk. Scalpel please. Have you ever seen an autopsy? The tissue and the meat give in so gallantly to the sterilized steel.
There was some sort of elemental fear always, afterwards, of infestation with maggots, or contamination of the wound. Yellow puss. Discharge. Scabbing.
Molysomophobia. Fear of infection.
And then I dreamt of leeches.
Crime scene cleaners.
It's so much easier to forgive the hitting.
The caseworker scribbles down things frantically. I tell her what she wants to hear. Give her lifelines. Bits and pieces. And I find myself feeling sorry for her. Feeling good that I'm helping her.

Making progress. Her progress. With me. Isn't it always like that? We just want to make people feel good.

She says, what about religion.

I don't know it well.

She says, but you quote the Bible. Always.

I tell her I have a good memory.

She says, what about God?

I say I've given that up for Lent. She laughs. No, really.

No, really.

She laughs.

Part of my job as her case number is to keep her entertained.

But no. I don't believe in you.

Him.

Her.

Me.

Anyone.

Twenty-Two
(Oui)

My agent comes back electronically. He says, we need to sexy up the story. We need more conflict. We need to get me in shape if we are going to be on television. We need some sort of consummation with Tramby Quirke. Consummation: the ultimate end. We need to stop talking in WCs. We need to chisel me into a sellable product. We need to negotiate a deal for my kin.
"Skin?"
No, kin. Only I have none.
My agent says, then we need to get you some.
We.
Drop fifteen pounds. Spend time under a giant lamp in the quest for that Georgie Porgie Hamilton tan. Hit the treadmill. Every night, climb up the Empire State Building.
My agent says, he's smuggled in syringes of Dianabol. And other steroids. And herbal remedies.
We.

We do them all. Meaning me. Me does them all: Arginine, ornithine, smilax, Inosine, DHEA, chromium, selenium, saw palmetto, orchid extract, ground down sheep testicle.

We move to the Chinese. We. But only me.

Tangkuei, Paonia, Cnidium, Scute, Gardenia, Forsythia, Siler, Schizonepeta, Chih-ko, Platycodon, Angelica, Bupleurum, and Licorice.

What we need now is a chemical peel.

Dandelion, Chrysanthemum wild, Isatis Radix, Baphicacanthus Leaf.

And yes; syringes of D-ball.

I say, what about my testicles? My agent says I won't need those.

"Tramby?"

He thinks.

"We'll work on that," he says.

We.

He says, we need to get you looking great. Pumped and ripped. Alert. Looking like a man.

Anadrol. Anabolic steroid. Synthetic derivative of testosterone. Possible side effects: impotence, chronic priapism, increased or decreased libido, insomnia, hair loss. Testicular atrophy.

Again I say, what about my nuts.

"We'll work on that, but for now, we need to get going on your face."

We.

Twenty-Three
(Hospitals)

The most attractive thing about being ripped to shreds in one-eighth of a second, is avoiding the requisite trip to the hospital. To the operating room. Intensive care. Hospice. Any of that and all of that. And if you can set it up so that you could do it live, or even On Demand television, then you've blasted two hummingbirds with one large stone. You end a contemptuous farce of a life, and you validate your former miserable, anonymous existence by turning into sellable, viable, astronomically-rated product: a high Q-score. You're on television. And that's the only thing that counts. It doesn't matter why or how. It's as much a compulsive habit as pornography.

Cigarettes.

Heroin.

D-ball.

Internet.

Narcissism as hopeless addiction. My caseworker says there are people specializing in treating that. I say, what. Say what? Narkisos. Thank you, Ovid.

I'm not perfect. Everyone has a weak side. Some of us have several.

My advanced directive: do not cut open the body. Though now it will be obsolete, the piece of signed and notarized paper. I loathe hospitals.

Staphylococcus aureus.

That spherical bacterium, frequently living on the skin or in the nose of a healthy person, that can cause a range of illnesses from minor skin infections (such as pimples, boils, and cellulitis) and abscesses, to life-threatening diseases such as pneumonia, meningitis, endocarditis, Toxic Shock Syndrome, and septicemia.

Before my mother put a proper hole in her chest with the family carbine, she submitted to the medical version of strapping a grenade to your breast and pulling the pin.

Double mastectomy.

The night-shift nurse withheld her Demerol for the first 12 hours, hoarding the medication for a later sale down U-Street Cardozo to some depressed housewife from the suburbs, driving an E-Class. There was no placebo effect and the carved out cancer-patient endured a shift's worth of excruciating pain. It was proven in a court of law.

Thank you, but no thank you.

Wire: Innocent and in a sense I am guilty of the crime that's now in hand.

How I feel is, Gram-positive. You know that...from Biology class.

Twenty-Four
(Where The Story Ends)

(alternate take)

In Studio 3B. In front of three robotic cameras, operated from a control room 240 miles away, in Secaucus, New Jersey. No one else with me except the A2. Two lousy souls in an empty office building. The A2. Nervously looping the lav mic and running it under my jacket, and up to the lapel. As if I have anything more to say. I ask again about the reel-to-reel tape and he says he's got it covered. (He thinks: Luddite!) My life in a messenger bag. He says to wait ten minutes after he leaves the studio. He says to wait for my cue in my ear.

Ten minutes. It's enough time to take the elevator down nine floors, leisurely walk out into the lobby, past the guard post, and into perpetual anonymity. A lousy social security number. A bar code. A treadmill. An item.

How I feel is, exploited. By my own doing. By others. Filling holes. Taste the iron in your blood. I cut myself because I didn't know what else to do. I cut with cold blades. I cut. Do you hear me. I cut because I didn't want to give anymore to anyone. No one could have me. That's why I cut. And became this. A spectacle.

I know in the control room, two states away, the TD is shuffling through his sequence of graphics. Lower thirds. Chyron. Double-boxes. The A2 has me in cue. Listening to my breathing pattern. My heart. The lavs are sensitive enough to pick up the thumps.

The munitions expert.

He says, when I pull the ripcord, there will be a quick flame from the ignition. That's all I'll see.

Fifty-one million people are watching this live.

After me, there will be a push for Friday Night Executions.

Blood as an addiction.

After me, the ratings will top the Dow.

All there's left is a digital clock counting time and frames.

30 per second.

My agent will move on to the next pariah cum preacher cum residual.

I hear the control room in my IFB.

This segment sponsored by.

Another product. New AND Improved — a linguistic impossibility. Everybody sells something. We're all marketers. Narcissistic egomaniacal broken down bolts. I'm done. I'm stripped.

down to black

roll eleven

up eleven

track eleven

5 move

(a remote camera arcs around)

insert

lose it

ready dissolve 3

dissolve

ready boxes

take boxes

(chatter of experts)

ready cue RS1

cue

insert

lose it

ready boxes

take boxes

(chatter)

RS2

take RS2

insert

RS3

RS2-take

ready RS3

RS3-take

boxes

boxes-take

(chatter, laughter)

RS2-take

insert

lose it

cue RS4

(Master cues me into my IFB)

RS4-take

I don't see the instant flame when I pull the ripcord.

alex m. pruteanu

end

interview with the author

This interview appeared in the September 2011 issue of *Gloom Cupboard* magazine, as part of *The New Хорошо* — a series by T. M. De Vos.

Reprinted with permission.

Alex Pruteanu is the author of Short Lean Cuts, a novella which, amongst other topics, explores the ever-escalating narratives offered for public consumption. Fittingly, my acquaintance with Pruteanu developed online and progressed via Facebook, the ultimate forum for constructed narratives of life and self. A native of Romania, familiar of Moldova, and American of thirty years, Pruteanu isn't waving a flag for any country, citing the natural clusters forming "villages, towns, or even cities" as the real loci of our allegiance. To quote Gogol Bordello, "Between the borders, the real countries hide." In the following interview, Pruteanu, the second featured author in "The New Хорошо," echoes the sentiment that the "the programmed robots are buying and buying" and shares his thoughts on place, nostalgia, timelessness, and how bestand will eventually snuff the human species.

GC: I found Chapter Twelve (Bestand) to be the crux, ideologically. For me, it spoke to the ethic of the extreme that is so ruthlessly bled in American media. The audience's compassion fatigue seems to require that entertainment escalate into caricaturish intensity: soon, there will be no crazy shit left to do. Even our own wounds as human beings have to be shocking enough, or we're not interesting, as creative people, as friends, as partners. I'm also imagining the environmental implications of this attitude; perhaps not imagining, really, because I think they're pretty evident. Can you say more about what bestand means to you as an author and as a human being (if those two roles are indeed different)?

AP: There are several ideas I examine in this novella. Consumerism is one of them. The word bestand literally means to stand around or about, beset, surround, to harass. Cognate with the German, bestehen, which means to subsist/to endure, and this is where Martin Heidegger's concept, or take on bestand initially caught my eye. At the time I wrote Short Lean Cuts, I was reading Heidegger's explorations of the question of Being and came across his idea that people tend to look at the world as a giant warehouse stocked with material ready for them to use; simple inventory available to be processed into something more valuable. Examples such as natural gas/petrol refined and re-sold, coffee beans ground down into fine espresso (commodities), trees shredded and manufactured into pulp and later into paper, animals mass-processed into unrecognizable foodstuff...basically products derived from natural resources. For those "have-nots" without access to the heavy-duty inventory like oil wells, diamond mines, natural gas pockets, it seems evolutionary to utilize the only thing they can tap: their own bodies or lives; their own intellectual property; their experiences as product; as entertainment, but as you say, as entertainment pushed to its ultimate limit—into "caricaturish intensity." What Heidegger points out in his theory is the tendency to translate bestand into exploitation and enslavement for our own benefit.

I see Heidegger's concept and its repercussions present in nearly every aspect of my daily life here in the States.

GC: Do you think that this issue of bestand is geographically, or temporally, inflected? Is bestand an original sin of being human, or is it possible for cultures—and individuals—to be less guilty?

AP: I think the tipping point (of no return) has been reached. Given the rapid population increase globally and the rapidly-decreasing resources, we are in for a miserable upcoming half of a century. I think humanity is glib enough to wipe itself off the face of this planet—whether via nuclear warfare or just systematically starving/satiating itself. I think it doesn't much matter what austerity measures we employ from now on (if they can even be legislated or passed as legislation), we are on the downside of the curve. I think it's too late.

From the obvious environmental impact of multinational corporations (extraction, seed re-engineering, genetically-modified organisms), to personal exploitation on national stages such as "reality shows," to every day exposition and narcissism on social networks such as Facebook, Twitter, and Google +. I want to underscore that among everything and everyone satirized in this novella, I include myself. I stress that self criticism in these following not-so-subtle lines the main character confesses in chapter twelve (Bestand): "And so this is what this is. This story. It's a shameless exploitation of my life; where everything becomes manufactured with a purpose: sell it to you."

And to get back to our discussion, let's be honest here: I am an author, peddling a product: a book. I want to sell that; to many people, in fact. In this way I, myself, am not above Heidegger's idea of "bestand," for as one of those "have-nots" I am utilizing the only thing I possess to reach into: my own experience, my own life turned into a product. It's quite refreshing and exhilarating to come clean in this way. I imagine this must have been what F. Scott Fitzgerald often felt, while methodically eviscerating his generation in literature and, most importantly, his own (parasitical) social class. But then again maybe I should exercise a bit more humility and not place myself in Fitzgerald's company or assume I have anything in common with him.

GC: Heh. Why do you suppose the "have-nots" and their misadventures are so marketable? Who are the consumers for this product?

AP: The consumers are the "have-nots" ourselves. Commiseration gives us a sense of camaraderie, but it also naturally flows into immiseration—the view that the nature of capitalist production logically requires an ever greater reduction in real wages and worsening of working condition for the middle or working class. It isn't just a Marxist thesis any longer; it's what's happening right now in the United States. All who refuse to see that are either blind, or speculating for a superior position.

You are correct when you decree: "soon there will be no crazy shit left to do." I wholeheartedly agree with that. I am waiting for the day when "Friday Night Executions" will take over the #1 spot on some network. You know, that Schwarzenegger movie "Running Man" doesn't seem all that farfetched now, does it?

GC: I haven't seen it. As a kid, I wasn't allowed to watch most movies or TV shows, and my efforts to break out of that mode of being (Dasein?) are spotty at best. I'll have to queue it.

AP: The basic premise is a futuristic TV game show in which the "contestants" are convicted criminal "runners" who must escape death at the hands of professional killers. It's set in 2017, and loosely based upon a Stephen King novel. We're not that far off from this premise. We're bored with most everything else; the stakes will more than likely be raised. And the ratings will follow. This is one of the ideas satirized in Short Lean Cuts; the extremism required for obtaining a high Q score.

GC: I always get fascinated by the wrong things, in books movies, people, places, and so on. Towards the end of Chapter Fifteen (Good Therapy), as you're listing the Latin names for esoteric phobias (I liked Bolshephobia, myself), I became hung up on the following passage:

> *Coimetrophobia—fear of cemeteries.*
> *Wrong. I've always loved them. I once read a book over satellite phone to a girl with blue eyes, in a cemetery. In another country. But I've locked that. That one is for me. I won't tell you about it.*

It's such an interesting act of defiance when the narrator gives this skeleton of the story but withholds the rest. What's locked here, for him?

AP: Again, Short Lean Cuts—among other things—is my attempt at criticizing our prevalent, skewed sense of self-importance, entitlement, and narcissism.

This is fundamentally the story of a man who will do anything to get a little face time (a high Q score, as it's used in television). It's also the story of crossing the line into becoming a product or a brand—again measured by a Q score—and exploited by various parasitical professions, such as psychiatrists, talent agents, or television producers. And one's own self (or one's id, un-checked by one's super-ego).

GC: I can see talent agents and television producers. I'm curious about your inclusion of psychiatrists in the parasite class. Do you view the other "helping professions" as harboring parasites on the have-nots?

AP: I have to be careful here that I don't sound like a Scientologist; I see and categorize most of the psychiatry discipline as a parasitical symbiotic relationship with its patients, yes. But please note the word "most" here. I view most of the medical system in the United States in much the same way. Again, I point to the word "most." This opens up a brand new Pandora's box of tangents and personal beliefs, but we may have to save that for another day. But since we're onto this, I also view the financial/banking system, in particular the Central Bank model, as a parasitical institution onto the working class, again engaged in a symbiotic relationship. The paralyzing effect of debt on our society in the States is yet another form of Heidegger's "bestand" theory.

I felt that the particular case in which the character withholds a personal story might add a bit to his complexity, and might humanize him a bit more. Here's a man consumed by narcissism (and perhaps large parts of mental illness, paranoia, etc.), but not completely yet. This story he holds for himself. Maybe this is the last thing he has that's his own that hasn't become a product; a Lifetime movie of the week. It just rounds this character a bit more. I don't necessarily think it makes him more like-able, however. And that's good. He is us, now, in the 21st Century…tweeting/Facebook-ing our location, our every move, our every bodily function. I don't like that. I don't like us.

GC: Valerie of Trick w/a Knife says that you have "mastered constructive nihilism." I am a huge nihilist and, like any fanatic, I love it when anyone else is. Are you? How the hell have you mastered it?

AP: I have always closely associated my belief in nihilism with existentialism. I first came upon the existentialists around age 16 or thereabouts. I don't quite remember how I bumped into the likes of Camus, Sartre, and Baudrillard—probably as a logical progression or a tangent of reading Kafka, but I did. I recall combining reading "The Stranger" with listening, at the time, to Pink Floyd's "The Wall" and "The Final Cut" and in my mind then, the two—existential literature and Floyd's two concept works—just seemed to fit nicely. It was around the same time I discovered the absurd theatre (Eugene Ionesco), so the trifecta was complete. I suppose I formed my initial thoughts on nihilism based upon my love and my identification with those first-encountered works; as well as a healthy dose of teenage angst and gloom and doom, naturally. But over the decades since, I feel I have never really strayed away from that belief base. That isn't to say I haven't progressed or understood logic better…in fact it's exactly because of that I still hold strong to my existential roots.

I think a lot of people mistake nihilism with a belief in nothing. I may be wrong about its meaning, but my belief is, indeed, in something: that everything is without objective meaning, purpose, or intrinsic value. I suppose I can be also shoved into the "moral nihilist" pig pen as well, as I also believe morality doesn't inherently exist, and that any established moral values are abstractly contrived. I pause here to chuckle at one of my favourite quotes from the eternal Oscar Wilde: "Morality is simply the attitude we adopt toward people we personally dislike."

GC: There aren't so much moral imperatives from on high as there are general agreements so that we can tranquilize Eros and Thanatos enough to live reasonably peacefully with others. Actions, really, aren't so much objectively good or bad as they are harmful or beneficial to one being or another. Your opinion on them depends on your relationship to the subject.

How do you distinguish the protagonist of a story under these circumstances? The antagonist or antagonizing forces?

AP: I don't distinguish him or her. Or at least I try not to. I am drawn to characters that exist somewhere in between those lines; the anti-heroes. I think it all started for me after first seeing Martin Scorsese's "Taxi Driver" sometime in my teens. Travis Bickle, for me, is the quintessential modern American anti-hero—whether in film or literature. I think of the narrator in Short Lean Cuts as Travis Bickle's natural descendant; the son Travis never had.

Jean Baudrillard has called postmodernity a nihilistic epoch and many figures of religious authority have decreed that postmodernity and many aspects of modernity represent a rejection of theism, and that such a rejection entails some form of nihilism. I couldn't agree more.

I don't believe I have mastered anything, much less the doctrine of disambiguation. But my writing is peppered with ideas of despair and a perceived pointlessness of existence that many readers seem to recognize and perhaps give meaning to, or work out on their own. In most cases, my stories have no clear ending, if any at all.

GC: Reading your blog, I was struck by how grounded your work is in place. Some places reverberated with all-Americanness, only to reveal that what an American reader might see as familiar is actually deeply bizarre or disturbing. Forgive me for pulling the nationality card, but how closely do these revelations fit with your own experience of American culture?

AP: Ever since arriving in the States in 1980 I've felt trapped between two countries. I've felt I never really had a good, long chance to develop any allegiance or patriotism for my country of birth, Romania, but at the same time—or rather, subsequently—I've also felt a nonchalance for my adopted country (the U.S.), and a lack of identification with any fundamental cultural or social aspect or movement in the United States—basically, I don't belong in either country, if anywhere at all. This is probably not something many people are used to hearing, and probably not something you were hoping to extract from me, when you initially decided to do this interview.

GC: It's really okay. This column is for the purposes of discussion, not flag-waving. You don't need to be a cultural artifact.

AP: It's hard to say whether or not, given more time to live in Romania, I would have developed a sense of loyalty in the first place. I find borders and divisions of land into countries or states or territories quite comical and absurd. To look on a map of the world and trace the lines which divide Tanzania from Kenya or from Burundi or Rwanda, or to see how natural geography such as lakes or rivers divide appropriated land is preposterous to me.

If anything, villages, towns, or even cities are the living breathing entities which theoretically could be partitioned, but anything larger than that, being divided and labeled in some way, and then administered by some sort of central government or government-like body, is incongruous.

That being said, I think my fiction naturally has that duality within it: perhaps a tinge of nostalgia for the country I knew my first 11 years of life, coupled with the "all-American-ness" of which you speak. But the finished product (story/novel/poem), I agree, is something that leaves the reader feeling uneasy and at times disoriented; something that is, as you say, "bizarre or disturbing." I think that is spot on, because for me as the writer, the feeling of being suspended in between two countries yields that sort of perspective. I think it challenges the reader to find meaning in that, and to examine his or her own ideas of what patriotism or allegiance really mean.

GC: There does seem to be a collusion in the clusters that make up the life of a small town, or even a large city, that isn't permeated by the political. When you feel nostalgia for Romania, do you feel nostalgic for the country, or for your own experience in the small society that enfolded you as a young child?

AP: I fight nostalgia with as much vigor as I can—both in my daily life, as well as in my fiction, but that isn't to say it doesn't slip into my stories…it's all right, however; I try to allow just enough to give some sort of emotion to these pieces, otherwise I might as well have a robot create them. Readers need to feel some emotional connection. To answer your question, I feel a combination longing for both the geography of the country, as well as my experiences and events surrounding them.

GC: Your pieces set in Eastern Europe seem to emerge on your blog every few posts. I noticed that they tend to be written from a distance of many years, which gives them a mood reminiscent of looking at an old scar or visiting the site of a historical tragedy. How does setting affect your tone, and your sense of time, when writing?

AP: Again, you are absolutely spot-on about these stories. They read like that because, in fact, they are written by a man who is standing on a far away shore, looking back. I try to remove all melancholy from these pieces in particular, when I write them, but there's no way to mask the distance from which I'm revisiting certain events and certain settings. They are subjective, and my view on the geography or time frame of a piece is quite subjective, but ultimately I am more interested in digging up and presenting the human condition under various circumstances — usually futile circumstances. These pieces don't seem to resonate with North American readers as much, or if they do, no one is commenting, and so I may have the wrong idea, but these stories are part of what I know and who I am. And little details that pop up, like Trabant cars, or eating stuffed cabbage leaves (sarmale) at Christmas time, are my homage to a slice of culture in which I was brought up. But they serve more as details or accoutrement to the central theme of the stories — which is usually isolationism, or an obtuse sense of not belonging anywhere.

In my head, Eastern European settings in my stories exist within the specific timeframe of the 1970s, but I write them carefully enough not to overtly place them there. The greatest thing about Communism is its ability to eradicate history, and effectively arrest time. (Walk around Havana lately?) If a writer is careful enough, that temporal permanence can be used to a great advantage as a framework for the intended purpose or idea of a story/novel, and not necessarily date it. It can work like a simple, wooden stage where only the play that is being acted upon it matters.

GC: That's an interesting idea—to present an ongoing dynamic about power—its wielding and abuses—and the banal, sort of poignant things people do and have done for generations—grow up, fall in love, look for community, lose people—despite whatever else may be going on around them. Are there other contexts, as well as Communism, that can create this effect of timelessness in a story—or, more accurately, this lack of location in time?

AP: Offhand I cannot think of anything else that doesn't enter into the science fiction rubric. I'm not well-versed in the sci-fi genre, so I may be wrong here. I suppose any repressive regime with the double-edged blade of eviscerating religion from the fabric of its society can work just as well. I've always found it fascinating that the most successful and longest-lasting dictatorships or repressive regimes are the ones that are based upon, or invoke a religious dogma. In fact, the process of answering this question has maybe yielded a response for you: Religion. Religion as an instrument of timelessness…or the eradication of temporal consciousness (offhand I can think of the Amish, in this country). Religion as the nullification of history; or science. Maybe that's where the Communists failed; maybe imposing atheism on society was the fundamental flaw.

One of my favourite writers is the recently-deceased, Nobel Prize winner Jose Saramago. In most of his works, he inserts allegories into un-named cities, un-named countries, and un-specified times (although most of his novels are dystopian by label). In fact, Saramago doesn't even bother with proper names, and so we get to follow the fate of The Blind Woman or The Grandmother or The Government Functionary.

GC: You commented on Facebook that your father, and you, are from Moldova, a country very close to my heart. What was it like to grow up there? How often do you get back? What's your take on Transnistria?

AP: I may have rushed with my comments (as I often do on Facebook) and may have been misunderstood; my father was born in a small village in Moldova, but I was born in Bucharest. However, I spent many a summer and winter at my father's place of birth while a young boy. In fact, during a brief time in 1977 after a major earthquake nearly leveled Bucharest, I attended school in my father's village. It is there that I got to see the Christmas ritual of my grandfather slaughtering the pig, and the simple, frugal, peasant way of life so many people here in the States talk about eventually recapturing.

GC: I always hear that kind of talk with a heavy dose of skepticism. How well do you think Americans would do at scaling back their bestand to that degree?

AP: I always apply a heavy coat of skepticism as well. I don't have faith that most Americans would do well under austerity measures of any kind. We are comfortable people now, more likely to start a revolution over the cancellation of the Super Bowl, than a legitimate cause. We are what I like to call "armchair supporters" of issues; that is to say, we'd much rather "thumb-up" on Facebook a movement or a crusade for (or against) something, than actually act upon it. So no, I have no faith that we, Americans, can voluntarily consume less. We will deplete everything before we even think about that.

I haven't been back since I left in 1980. Since then, my father's parents have passed away and the family house has been taken over and re-modeled by my cousin, her husband, and my uncle (her father). The house now has running water, a telephone, and almost all the modern amenities one would expect. The dirt roads of the village have been paved. Strangely, I am not in a hurry to get back and take in all the progress, or re-connect in any way. I am probably a rare case of an expatriate who doesn't get too sentimental about concepts such as "homeland" or "Mother Country" or even geography in general. While I adore and appreciate nature and geographical features, I don't feel any particular calling to it. My father, also a writer, has been back numerous times in the last thirty-one years, and that part of the world features prominently in his novels. In fact, his latest book is set in his home village and features as the main character my daughter, in an allegorical return to the homeland to be raised by a handful of strange and wonderful characters—all natives of the village.

GC: I don't mean to ask the most obvious questions, but here I go anyway: how much influence has your father being a writer influenced your own path? Would an overly deterministic reader detect any filial strain/conversation/rebellion in your father's, and your, writing styles? And what titles would an overly deterministic reader look up on, say, her Nook or other e-reading device to find out?

AP: I probably began to write because I was an only child in Romania and most of the fantastic worlds that existed for a young boy were found in books. And so I spent a lot of free time reading. I suppose that was a direction that my father encouraged, he being a writer, but I'd say my mother equally influenced that development. Or maybe it was just situational. We didn't have entertainment on TV or much at the cinema.

As I got older, and came to the States, my father always supported my path as a writer, but he hasn't had much stylistic influence on my own work at all. He is a much more classical, ornate kind of writer; he loves similes and metaphors, and he draws heavily from cultural/local myth and folklore as well as world philosophy. My father is much better read in, for example, Eastern philosophy than I am. Stylistically, I am less interested in allegory and symbolism—both which feature prominently in my father's writing, and more concerned with the humanity—or loss thereof—of my characters placed within a modern setting or world. I would classify my father as a brilliant story teller, able to draw from the Romanian folklore and spin fantastic tales. He was also a working actor while in Romania, so he has quite the ability to deliver these tales. I don't believe his work is available to purchase on electronic devices. All of his novels are written in Romanian and have been published and distributed in Romania only. Aside from the personal copies he's distributed to family and friends here, I believe you can only purchase his novels from the publishers themselves.

On Transnistria I can only say that, like other post-Soviet frozen conflict zones such as Abkhazia and South Ossetia, I hope the international community will eventually recognize it as an independent state.

GC: How much do you follow the politics in that region? How does your stance on morality affect your reaction to the social issues there—such as discrimination against the Roma and human trafficking, for example?

AP: Yes, I tend to stay interested and pretty well connected to that side of our world via news outlets and occasional interaction with friends or distant family. There is discrimination against everyone by virtually everyone—historically and elementally—

within humanity. No atrocity can shock me any longer...not at my age. I am able to see both sides in the Roma/Gypsy situation. Neither side is necessarily clean or ethical in their generalizations or actions. I don't believe in that "can't we all just get along?" rhetorical bullshit. It's been historically proven that we cannot. I can basically infer that we will not ever be able to. I'm not necessarily a squeaky-clean, ultra-ethical person either, so I cannot truly and honestly decree anything, or deem myself anything. In the exploitation of Man by Other Man I can only nod my head and acknowledge that it will never stop. It is how we are.

GC: And how did you get to North Carolina?

AP: Through a mélange of fortunate and unfortunate events, my journey from Romania took me to Cleveland, Washington D.C., a brief stop in Los Angeles, south Florida, a quick flirtation with Toronto, and finally the research triangle area (Raleigh/Durham/Chapel Hill) in North Carolina. The story is too long to tell here; even I couldn't compress thirty-one years in one paragraph, but suffice it to say I am quite content with co-existing in this part of the country. I have fairly quick access to family in Washington D.C. and south Florida, as well as proximity to New York City, Atlanta, and even New Orleans if I feel the need to visit or go on short holiday.

GC: Your reviewers wax pretty lyrical about diamonds amid dross, slashing scalpels, and punches in the face. The word "dark" also came up a lot. What about your writing has such a visceral effect on people?

AP: Dark is good. It's nothing to be afraid of. I love the recent discovery of dark, rogue planets floating freely in space, not ensnared by the gravity of a star or a particular solar system, but

I digress. I think the writing is what the reader says it is. In fact, re-reading through the final copy of the Short Lean Cuts manuscript I found myself bursting into laughter many times. I'm not sure that's a by-product of "something dark" but again, it is what the reader says it is.

GC: As a reader of your own work, what would you say it is?

AP: I'd say this particular novella certainly explores some of the nastiest, seediest sides of our private lives or thoughts or fetishes. And the short, sharp, poking style in which it's written definitely adds to a sort of urgent undercurrent that flows throughout the book—it's all leading pretty quickly to an end of some sort; whether real or imagined. But again, reading through the final manuscript I found myself laughing quite often. I think there are parts that are hilarious in this book. Maybe that doesn't make me too normal.

I learned the mechanics of writing in English by reading Ernest Hemingway initially. I was attracted to the enormous amount of feeling and complicated emotion living within (or hidden by) deceptively sparse language. We all know how much Hemingway revolutionized the written English language, but I don't think we realize just how many writers and artists he influenced. I think his reach into an artist's brain is gargantuan—whether conscious or not. One of my favourite writers, Hunter S. Thompson, used to sit down at his desk, while learning how to write, and type out passages from Hemingway's novels in order to learn pacing.

And so, having English as my second language, I was immediately attracted to a simpler, less Dickensian or Proustian kind of style. But I also was attracted by what was being said, or rather, left out…and how much of it there was. Yes, I see delivering sentences similar to delivering jabs or upper cuts or hooks to the ribs, but never to simply shock…or as a gimmick. I also think that style works to my advantage in this time when people have shorter attention spans and will not hang in with long, verbose passages or novels. Expostulation of ideas in hundreds of thousands of words does not interest me. My ideal novel is eighty or so thousand words.

I think readers are attracted to this style because it delivers that punch without mucking about for too long. I spend quite some time choosing and picking simple language that carries and delivers much more that what's on the surface, and often times I re-write quite a bit—most of the time looking to cut and cut some more. I once kidded with a writer friend that one day I'll have this science down to basically not writing anything at all. The manuscript will be one nice, neat, blank page; everything distilled down to nothing. That will be the scam of the century. P.T. Barnum will be proud of me. And I will sell that to many.

GC: The perfect nihilist novel. Wasn't there a musician whose entire performance was the sounds of the audience as they shuffled around, waiting for the show to start?

AP: I don't know, but that sounds like a piece of "music" I'd be drawn to.

GC: What was some of the material you cut: background about the character, additional scenes or relationships, more inner musings, a longer stretch of time, other?

AP: In fact, with this book I ended up adding material, bridging the chapters with unifying details to round out the story. I originally had the idea of writing each chapter as a piece of flash fiction that would be able to stand alone if chosen to be published as such, as well as serve as support for a larger story. In pulling all the chapters together, I found it necessary to fuse them into a more coherent, general idea. Because of the revisions I did, I think at this point one is no longer able to pluck out the chapters and have them stand independently. That being said, I think this particular style of writing will grate on a reader's brain if experienced for too long—and so this is exactly why I decided Short Lean Cuts should be a novella. I cannot imagine it being any longer than that.

GC: You commented about your recording of "May Day" for Pank that you found that "author readings take away some things from a piece." What do you feel is lost, in general? What was lost from "May Day" as a result of this recording?

AP: Actually, I think my reading of "May Day" in Pank did the piece quite the justice it deserved. In general I find that for me, authors reading their works take away from the dynamic or the intensity of the passage they're reciting. Either the author is reading in such an affected manner or with such a grave cadence that it literally makes me laugh and distracts me from the work itself, or—as is the case with some younger authors I've heard—they rush through their pieces, often times up-talking (ending every sentence as a question) and, again, taking focus away from their written work.

GC: That manner of speaking? Totally seems? To be, like, the curse of today's youth? You know what I mean?

AP: I do, I do…it's precisely that sort of cadence that distracts me from the piece that's being read. But you know, that was "the curse" of my youth as well…remember in the early 80s Moon Zappa had that hit "Valley Girl." Totally, like…you know?

I remember, during my teenage infatuation with Hemingway's work, I once came upon a recording of him reciting some early poems he had written in the early 1920s and I was shocked at how morose, how affected, how serious he sounded. He even had a bit of a Queen's English accent—he being raised in the Michigan countryside. I was speechless. I began to laugh. I recall even saying out loud: how in hell can you take yourself so seriously, man? Fitzgerald was the same. Even though I adore Fitzgerald's writing, hearing him read just distracts me from the work—again, that classic, affected, upper-strata cadence that just kills me. Of course, I do understand Fitzgerald was upper class personified, so he may be allowed a pass.

I think we writers often take ourselves way too seriously. We all piss into the same porcelain pot, really. Let's stop with the shenanigans and pretension.

That being said, the best readings I've heard were Charles Bukowski reciting his poems. He always delivered in that laid-back, everything's cool, southern California manner, and he always had a little smirk on his face…alongside his bottle of wine, of course.

I do have to admit I don't like the "author reading from his work" model that bookstores seem to still employ, in order that they sell the product. I find that authors at the lectern reading, inserts some sort of divide between them and their audiences. I'd much rather attend a question-answer only session with an author, than sit quietly for upwards of an hour, hands in my lap, while the artiste showers me with his or her interpretation.

GC: What do you think of some of the alternatives to the traditional literary reading—for example, the "Brothellian Movement," wherein patrons buy one-on-one sessions with costumed poets, or scripted performance art/literature that involves the audience to varying degrees?

AP: I must admit before you mentioned it, I'd never heard of the Brothellian Movement. But it sounds comical to me. At that point, why not just have it be theatre? That being said, things like Renaissance festivals and war re-enactments are big here in the States. I'm not sure why, and I'd never attend any of them as I'm not interested in re-living the past, but that's just my personal preference. The thing that is probably the most creepy and bizarre to me is the Civil War re-enactments that go on here every year consistently. I truly don't understand those. Or any war re-enactment for that matter. Why are people interested in exploring strife and depravity and horrific death, or deplorable conditions? Why not move forward?

But to get back to your question, I suppose if an artist can make a living any which way he or she can, then it's quite acceptable to don tunics or tights and recite some poetry.

We are writers, not voice-over personalities. We should just write.

GC: This is in a different vein, perhaps, but what is your take on the industries that have grown up around writing, such as the MFA program and the Expensive Literary Retreat in a Nice Place? Local workshops and writers' groups are, I guess, their poor cousins. Why do you suppose so many people believe that they have poetry, or a novel, in them?

AP: Personally, I've never attended or have been part of such things…nor am I interested in any of them. My take on them is that they wouldn't have helped me more than just reading voraciously, in general. And writing. I suppose so many people believe that they have poetry, or a novel in them because they are misinformed by the ones who love them. Or they watch too many films that feature "the common man" suddenly being plucked from obscurity and recognized for that hidden, well-tuned talent. They are misguided and wrongly encouraged. I think there is nothing wrong with telling a family member or a friend that, despite his or her belief, he/she cannot write well. But...perhaps he/she can draw well, or sing well, or play an instrument well, or just be a good mother or father or husband or wife, etc. All of that is equally important in a life. One doesn't have to be an artist at all, to contribute positively to society. And...finally a cliché has found its way to the surface.

Made in the USA
Lexington, KY
15 March 2012